Reading Together

The Hairy Toe

D1312266

# Read it together

It's never too early to share books with children. Reading together is a wonderful way for your child to enjoy books and stories — and learn to read!

One of the most important ways of helping your child learn to read is by reading aloud — either rereading their favorite books, or getting to know new ones.

Encourage your child to join in with the reading in every possible way. They may be able to talk about the pictures, point to the words, take over parts of the reading, or retell the story afterward.

With books they know well, children can try reading to you. Don't worry if the words aren't always the same as the words on the page.

If they are reading and get stuck on a word, show them how to guess what it says by:
* looking at the pictures
* looking at the letter the word begins with
* reading the rest of the sentence and coming back to it.
Always help them out if they get really stuck or tired.

*... began to moan and ... What's next?*

*groan. "Moan" and "groan" are nearly the same, aren't they?*

Sometimes you can help children look more closely at the actual words and letters. See if they can find words they recognize, or letters from their name. Help them write some of the words they know.

**Which words do you know on this page?**

**Night, home, bed, Hairy Toe.**

*I liked all the cre-eak-ing.*

Talk about books with them and discuss the stories and pictures. Compare new books with ones they already know.

I liked it when the wind went **SWOOSH!** around the house.

We hope you enjoy reading this book together.

# For Kerris and Kitty

Illustrations copyright © 1998 by Daniel Postgate
Introductory and concluding notes copyright © 1998 by CLPE/L B Southwark

Second U.S. edition in this form 1999

Library of Congress Catalog Card Number 98-88094

ISBN 0-7636-0860-2

4 6 8 10 9 7 5

Printed in Hong Kong

Candlewick Press
2067 Massachusetts Avenue
Cambridge, Massachusetts 02140

# The Hairy Toe

## A Traditional American Tale

illustrated by
# Daniel Postgate

CANDLEWICK PRESS

Once there was a woman went out to pick beans,

and she found ...

a Hairy Toe.

She took the Hairy Toe
home with her,

and that night,
when she went to bed,

the wind began to moan and groan.

Away off in the distance
she seemed to hear
a voice crying,

"Where's my Hair-r-ry To-o-o-oe?
Who's got my Hair-r-ry To-o-o-oe?"

The woman scrooched down,

way down

under the covers,

and about that time,

the wind appeared to hit the house,

**SWO**

"Where's my
Hair-r-ry To-o-oe?

Who's got my
Hair-r-ry To-o-oe?"

The woman scrooched farther down

under the covers

and pulled them tight around her head.

The wind growled around the house,
like some big animal,

and **r-r-um-mbled**
over the chimbley.

All at once she heard the door **cr-r-a-ack**

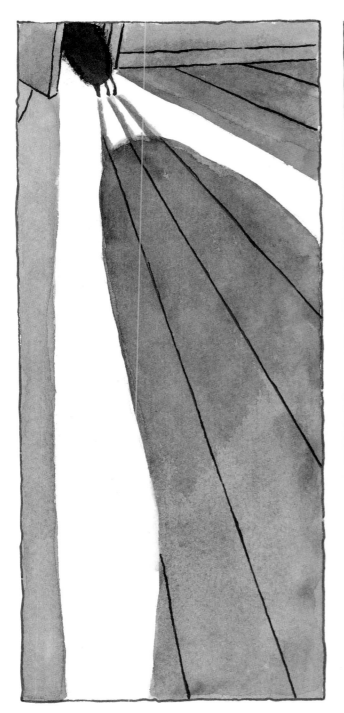

and Something
slipped in

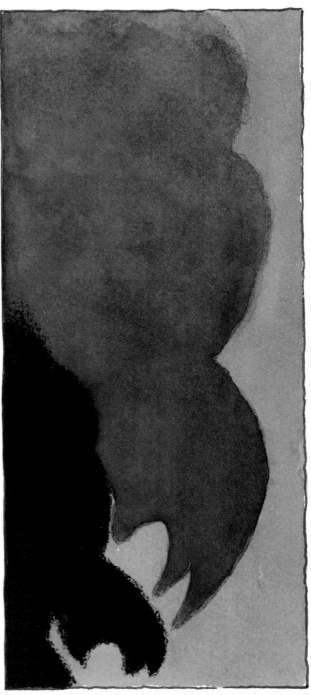

and began to creep
over the floor.

The floor went **cre-e-eak,** *cre-e-eak*

with every step Something took

toward her bed.

The woman could almost feel it bending over her bed.

Then in an awful voice it said,

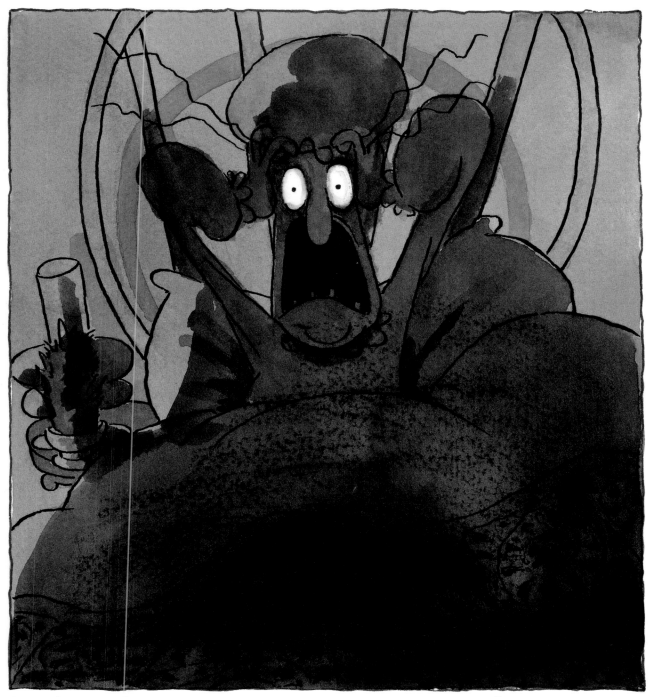

"Where's my Hair-r-ry To-o-oe?
Who's got my Hair-r-ry To-o-oe?"

# "You've got

# Read it again

## What would you do with a Hairy Toe?

A Hairy Toe is a strange thing to find in a field of beans, and it is very odd to take it home and keep it by the bed.
You can talk about why the old woman decided to keep it.
What would you have done with the toe?

I could wear it in my hat!

Maybe I should take it to the police ...

or give it to a museum.

## How did Something lose its toe?

We don't know how Something was separated from its toe. How do you think it happened? Children might imagine all kinds of different explanations.

Yikes!

Maybe a dog thought it was a bone and grabbed it.

Yummy!

A bird tried to take it to her nest but it was too heavy.

## Tell the story

Children can use the pictures to retell the story. They can make it as scary as possible by using their voice to build up suspense and by adding the noise of the howling wind and loud footsteps.

Swoosh!

And the old house crrr-e**aked** and crrr-a**cked**. . . .

## What makes it scary?

You can help your child think about what makes this a scary story. Look through the book together and talk about all the scary parts in the story and pictures.

Those shadows are really creepy.

## Scary stories

Make a list together of all the things you might find in a scary book. Children can write or draw their own scary stories. They could record them on a tape, perhaps adding sound effects. You could try writing a story yourself, and then suggest your child draw pictures to go with it.

Giant

Ghost

Witch

## Other tales

If this is a particular kind of story your child enjoys, you could look for other traditional tales about ghosts, giants, goblins, or witches. You may know other scary stories to tell.

# Reading Together

The Reading Together series is divided into four levels—starting with red, then on to yellow, blue, and finally green. The six books in each level offer children varied experiences of reading. There are stories, poems, rhymes and songs, traditional tales, and information books to choose from.

Accompanying the series is the *Reading Together Parents' Handbook,* which looks at all the different ways children learn to read and explains how *your* help can really make a difference!

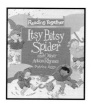